THE ADVENTURES OF CEDRIC THE BEAR

LUCIA WILSON   ANNE BOWES

KATIE EGGINGTON

ISBN: 9789493056176 (ebook)

ISBN: 9789493056169 (paperback)

Publisher: Amsterdam Publishers

info@amsterdampublishers.com

CONTENTS

PART 1

CEDRIC AT THE MUSEUM

INTRODUCTION

Well, hello! How lovely to see you-ooooo...

I was just having a snooze. In fact, I was dreaming about something that happened to me when I was a young cub. It really was quite an adventure!

Would you like to read all about it? Well, snuggle down, get nice and cosy and turn the page...

CHAPTER 1

One beautiful summer's day, Cedric was taken to a very special place because Cedric is a very special bear.

He is not covered in fur as you would expect, no, instead he is made from a unique material designed by an extremely clever lady called Katie.

Can you believe that Katie can turn balls of yarn into beautiful cloth? Yes, she can and she uses a very interesting piece of equipment called a loom, and with her loom she creates…. magic!

Katie weaves the yarn into fabric and all the beautiful threads blend together in a lovely, colourful pattern like the one for Cedric's coat – red, gold and yellow, the colours of autumn leaves.

When Katie and Cedric reached this special place, they met a team of important people.

The judges decided that Cedric was so unique and wonderfully crafted that he deserved to be displayed in a location where everyone could appreciate how fine he was – which is how Cedric ended up in the Victoria and Albert Museum in London! Isn't that wonderful?

One day, Cedric was sitting proudly in his personal glass case, watching all the visitors, some of whom were watching Cedric.

At the opposite end of the V&A shop were two young children, Julie and Freddie. Their mum, Alice, was busy talking to her friend, Georgina, so Alice didn't notice Julie pulling Freddie by the hem of his brand-new school jumper; she would have been extremely cross!

"Come on!" said Julie, "I want to see Cedric the bear!" as they gently pushed their way through the crowd.

"Oh, he's cool," said Freddie.

Freddie liked saying 'cool'.

"I think he's sooooo lovely," said Julie, who liked saying 'sooooo'.

"Do you think Mummy will buy him for us? Let's go back and ask her!"

They tried to run back to Alice but it was so crowded that it wasn't easy to move quickly and when they did reach their mummy, she was still talking to Georgina.

Freddie opened his mouth to speak but Julie looked at him and put her finger to her own mouth and said "shh".

They knew it was rude to interrupt grown-ups so they had to wait. Freddie was in agony!

Then Alice looked down, smiling, and said, "What is it, Freddie?"

"Mummy, please come and see Cedric! We want you to buy him!"

"Well, I'll come and look, but I am not promising anything!" she said with a laugh as they led the way.

But when they got to the glass case Cedric was gone!

"Oh, no!" cried Julie and Freddie.

Alice sensed that tears were not far away and she said quickly, "Never mind. Let's ask the shop assistant."

But when Alice approached the shop assistant who came to see the empty glass case, she was really shocked and turned to the shop manager, a fussy lady with huge spectacles whose eyes grew even bigger at the sight of the empty glass case.

"We must inform Security," said the shop manager solemnly.

She dashed to the telephone, and do you know

what happened next? They closed the museum and locked everyone in! One by one, everyone in the museum shop had to show what was in their bag before they could leave.

"Outrageous!" barked one pompous man.

"Quelle horreur!" cried a smart French lady.

"I haven't taken anything! I shall speak to my MP!" said a stylish woman with green hair.

"And I'm going to tell my Mum!" said a young boy who was also searched.

"Sorry, Ladies and Gentlemen, but we have to do this, standard procedure. Please move along, we must check everyone..." said the kind security guard, Max.

Julie and Freddie were at the back of the queue of people waiting to be searched.

"What do you think has happened, Freddie?" said Julie in a loud whisper.

"No idea, Jules, but isn't it exciting? Cool!"

Just then, Julie and Freddie noticed a tall young security guard, who had very slim arms and a big tummy. His tummy was so big that his jacket didn't really fit. He looked very strange.

"Do you mind if I just step outside for a bit of air? I feel queasy," said the tall guard.

Max, the older guard didn't look up as he was busy checking another bag. "Yes, yes," said Max and the young man turned around quickly. As he did this, one of the buttons on his tight jacket popped.

"Look, Freddie," said Julie in a whisper. "Has he got...? Is that...?"

"Yes! He's got Cedric!" said Freddie.

"Mummy, look! That guard..."

But Alice looked sternly at Freddie because she was speaking to Georgina about how this search was going to make her late for lunch with her husband's business partner. Freddie knew the rule about interrupting grown-ups but really, this was an emergency.

Freddie looked at Julie and she shrugged her shoulders in frustration.

They both looked again for the young guard, but he had disappeared.

CHAPTER 2

When Julie and Freddie got home, Mummy and Daddy went out again quickly as they were already late for their appointment.

Georgina was babysitting and switched on the children's TV channel for them whilst she prepared their lunch.

"Let's check the news," said Julie and took hold of the remote control to change the channel.

"And now, some breaking news from the V&A Museum. We can go to our reporter at the scene, Maria Gomez."

"Good afternoon. In the last few moments, we have been told that there has been a bear-napping at the V&A! I repeat, Cedric, the bear, has been taken! The museum has received a ransom message via email. Police are monitoring the situation closely. We will update you again on this fast-moving situation but in the meantime, if any members of the public know anything at all, please contact Scotland Yard immediately!"

"You see, Julie! We need to contact Scotland Yard immediately! Cedric's in danger!"

"But how do we contact Scotland Yard? We're not supposed to use the phone!"

They both thought very hard.

"I know," said Julie, "we need to speak to…"

"The Chief!" they said in unison.

"Okay, let's go," said Freddie, but just then Georgina placed a delicious lunch in front of them.

"… After lunch," he whispered.

And Julie just nodded her head because she was already eating.

Once they had finished their lunch, Julie and Freddie told Georgina they were going to play in the garden. Georgina said "okay" and carried on texting on her mobile.

When they were in the garden they opened the small wooden gate that led into the garden next door. They knocked on the window and waited.

After a few moments, they saw the smiling face of an old man leaning on a walking frame.

"Hello, Chief! We need your help… it's an emergency!" said Freddie in a serious voice.

"An emergency, eh?" said the Chief. "Come on in then and tell me all about it."

When Julie and Freddie finished telling their story, the Chief sat back and stroked his bristly chin. He was clearly thinking hard and Julie and Freddie watched him with wide eyes.

CHAPTER 3

Meanwhile, in a small flat in North London, Cedric was in a smelly portable kennel and the door was locked.

Through the wire door of the kennel, Cedric could see Troy Chambers bent over his computer. He was talking to himself. "Now they'll listen to me, they won't be able to ignore me any longer."

He sounded angry but also rather sad, a bit like a small boy even though he was a tall young man. Troy looked older than his fourteen years because of his height.

"What are you doing?" asked Cedric in a polite voice.

Troy turned and peered at Cedric. "I've sent a ransom note to the museum. I'm not going to let you go until they pay up."

Cedric thought about this. "Why are you angry with the museum?"

It was Troy who was thoughtful this time. "Well, I'm not really angry with the museum..."

"And who did you mean when you talked about someone listening to you?" interrupted Cedric.

"You ask a lot of questions for a bear!" shouted Troy.

"Well, you know, we are going to be together for quite a while it seems, so we might as well have a chat," said Cedric reasonably.

"It's the kids in my class! I'll show them. They keep telling me I'm rubbish and that they don't want to talk to me. They call me a freak because I'm so tall. And then, the other day, well, they said I was chicken, a coward and they said I would never do anything special or brave. They dared me to do something. They were laughing at me! So when I saw them cleaning your glass case at the museum, well..."

And suddenly Troy began to cry and he really did look more and more like a little boy. Embarrassed, Troy left the room.

Poor boy, thought Cedric, *people probably think he's so much older than he is because he's so tall. His classmates are rotten to call him names and to be so mean. I am sure he doesn't want to do anything bad to me but I really would like to go home!*

He looked around the kennel which was dirty and smelly and thought longingly of his own clean, bright and comfy room in Katie's house.

As Cedric brushed off some of the dirt, his hand touched the little identity button that Katie had created especially for him.

"But of course!" declared Cedric, "how silly of me to forget!"

He looked at the back of the button and turned on the tiny little switch. He had activated the microchip! Now Katie could track him on her mobile phone!

"Oh, I do love modern technology!" said Cedric

and smiled as Troy came back into the room carrying a tray.

"Would you like a biscuit?" said Troy in a small voice.

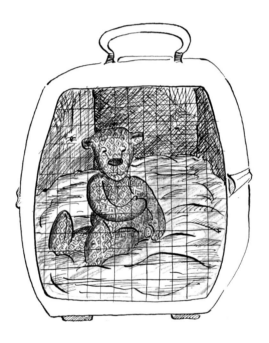

CHAPTER 4

Back at the Chief's house, Julie and Freddie were still waiting for the Chief's instructions.

"Right," he said decisively. "I need to call my old chum, Reggie in Scotland Yard."

A shiver of excitement ran down Freddie's neck like an ice cube down his shirt and this time it was Julie who said "cool!".

Julie then jumped up to pass the Chief his phone.

Both Julie and Freddie leant forward as the Chief spoke in brief, business-like phrases to his pal Reggie, also known as Chief Inspector Pickles of Scotland Yard.

"Cedric's been microchipped, you say? It's hidden

in his ID button? So that's how you tracked them down. Well, that's very handy! Witnesses? Yes, they're here with me. Good idea, I'll bring them along but you know, I can't get out easily these days, Reggie... my legs, you know..." He looked upset and a bit embarrassed, and then his expression cleared.

"Squad car on its way? Cheers, Reggie, we'll be ready!"

"Are we going in a squad car?" said Freddie, his eyebrows at the top of his head.

"Yep. Need to tell Georgina, first. Julie, you run round and get her."

Freddie threw himself backwards on the sofa and was too excited to even whisper 'cool!'

When the squad car arrived, the police officer, Sergeant Peters, showed Julie and Freddie some photos of the young man inside the flat.

"Now look closely, you two. Does this look like the same person you saw in the V&A Museum with Cedric?"

Carefully the children looked at the pictures and

they said yes it was the same person, although they hadn't realised he was just a teenage boy.

"Yes, he's very tall for his age but he's only fourteen," said Sergeant Peters. "He's not much older than my son," she said.

"Okay, let's go!" ordered Sergeant Peters.

The sound of the police siren and the flashing blue lights made Freddie and Julie jump and they both grabbed hold of the Chief's hands.

CHAPTER 5

Back at the flat, Troy was looking at his mobile phone. Cedric was straining to see what he was doing.

Then he heard a small sound, like a drop of rain onto glass.

Troy was crying again.

"Are you all right, Troy?" Cedric asked kindly.

"It's a text from my Mum. She said she's in a police car and they are coming to get me!"

He was crying hard now. "What am I going to do, Cedric? This has all gone too far! I only wanted to show those bullies at school that I'm not a coward!"

"Troy, can I tell you something? You shouldn't take any notice of bullies. Who cares what they think? I don't! Bullies are rotten and mean and you don't need friends like that. I know you didn't want to hurt me but it would be nice if you could let me out of this kennel. It really stinks!"

"Oh sorry, Cedric, sure," and he opened the door and lifted Cedric out.

"Now," said Cedric, "let's take a selfie and send it to your Mum and then to Katie," and Cedric put his arm around Troy's neck.

Troy smiled weakly into the camera.

"Now, Troy, just text this message: *Sorry, Mum, sorry, Katie, please come and get us. Cedric is fine, as you see. I will apologize to the police and the museum as well. I am really and truly very sorry. Troy.*"

"Call coming through for you, Sarg!" said PC Dawson handing her the receiver.

"Yes? I see, good," said Sergeant Peters. "Okay, Dawson, switch off the sirens."

"Why, Sarg, what's happened?" asked PC Dawson.

"Looks like the bear-napping is over. The kid's given himself up. His Mum's on her way and Katie is coming for Cedric."

"Okay, Sarg, we've arrived anyway."

Sergeant Peters turned to the Chief and said, "Thanks, Chief, for all your help, but we can take it from here. And as for you two," she looked at Julie and Freddie, "I'll be recommending you both for our *Good Citizen Award*, well done!"

"That's soooo cool!!" said Julie and Freddie together.

"Dawson, I'm going to speak to Troy and his Mum. I do need to have a serious chat with that boy. You drive the children and the Chief home and then meet me back at the station," said Sergeant Peters briskly as she got out of the car.

As PC Dawson began to turn the car around, Julie and Freddie said, "Oh, please wait! There's Cedric with Katie!"

Cedric and Katie were waving and smiling and the children jumped out of the car and gave Cedric a big hug. Everyone was chatting excitedly.

"Well, well," said the Chief, "I think we need to get you two home as it is well past your bed time I suspect!" as he finally managed to persuade the children back into the car.

"Oh, but I am not the least bit sleepy!" said Freddie with tired, wide eyes.

"Nor me!" said, Julie as she swallowed a yawn.

Five minutes later the Chief looked at the back seat and smiled; they were both fast asleep.

"So, Cedric, are you sure you are okay after your scary adventure?" said Katie as she drove back to her home.

"Oh, I was never really scared, Katie, I'm fine. As good as new!"

"Well, not quite good as new," said Katie, "if you don't mind me saying so, Cedric, I think you might need a bath... You smell terrible!"

And they both laughed and laughed.

THE END

PART 2

CEDRIC AND THE BUTTON BEAR

CHAPTER 1

"Help!"

Cedric looked all around but couldn't see anyone.

"I'm down here! Oh, please help me!"

Cedric looked down towards a basement window and noticed a strange… well, he wasn't sure what to call it. It was certainly an odd-looking creature whatever it was!

As Cedric looked more closely, he could make out two, very sad, big, brown eyes surrounded by lots of different buttons. How peculiar!

Cedric, who had a kind heart, spoke to the unhappy fellow, "How can I help you?"

"Look, there's not a lot of time, he's going to come back in a minute!"

"Who?"

"Mr Sparks, the tailor. He's so horrible! Do you see all of these buttons? Well, he stitches them onto me so that he doesn't lose them – and it hurts a lot I can tell you – and just look at the state of me! You wouldn't want to look like this, would you?"

"Well, no, but can I just ask..."

But just then the creature cried, "Oh, no, he's coming back!" and he closed the shutters abruptly.

"Wait!" said Cedric, but it was too late.

Cedric stayed there for a moment or two, wondering if the creature would open the shutters again but he didn't.

Cedric felt quite upset and really didn't know what to do next.

Then he decided to continue on his way to visit his friend Polo who lived at London Zoo. Polo was very clever, and Cedric decided to tell him all about the strange fellow in the tailor's basement.

Two heads are better than one, thought Cedric.

CHAPTER 2

"Hi, Polo! You look smart!"

"Thanks, Cedric. I'm just about to go on for the afternoon show."

Polo had a starring role in the Penguin Parade that took place every Thursday at the zoo.

"You look a bit worried, Cedric, what's up?" said Polo.

Cedric told Polo what had happened with the strange creature in the tailor's basement and Polo turned his head from side to side which is what he always did when he was listening carefully.

"I tell you what, Cedric, why don't you come and watch the parade and afterwards you and I can go back there together to see if we can help this poor fellow, okay?"

"Perfect! Thanks, Polo!"

Cedric thoroughly enjoyed the Penguin Parade and soon after he and Polo were heading back to the tailor's shop. Fortunately, the shutters were open, and Cedric and Polo could look inside; they took great care to make sure they were not seen. They could see Mr Sparks cutting buttons off an old jacket. Beside him was the strange individual that Cedric had met earlier that day.

"Ouch!" said the poor fellow as Mr Sparks stitched the buttons from the old jacket onto its body.

Cedric and Polo winced as they watched.

"What do you think it is, Polo?"

"Can't you tell, Cedric? I think he's one of your relations!"

Cedric looked again and opened his eyes wide. "Goodness me, it's a bear! It's hard to tell under all those buttons! I must help him, Polo. I've got to rescue him!"

"And I'll help you," said Polo. "Two heads are better than one!"

For a moment, Cedric and Polo were quiet. Polo turned his head from side to side whilst Cedric rested his chin on his chest, thinking very hard.

Then, before either of them could speak, they heard a door closing; it was the tailor. He seemed to be in a great hurry.

Cedric and Polo turned to the window and called down to the poor button bear.

"Quickly!" shouted Cedric. "Tell us how we can help you!"

"Oooh, thank you, thank you!" cried the button bear.

"Manners, Cedric, please. Introductions first," said Polo, straightening his bow tie with his flippers.

"My name is Polo, and this is Cedric. What's your name, please?"

The button bear looked very sad. "I don't have a name, or at least I don't think so. Mr Sparks just calls me the Button Bear."

"Oh, that's just too bad, that's awful!" said Polo.

"Yes, it really is," said Cedric, "but we do need to hurry up in case Mr Sparks comes back! Do you know where he's gone?"

"I think he's gone to the bank. I don't think he'll be very long. I know he has to finish a suit for a customer who is arriving later this afternoon."

"Okay, I've got an idea," said Cedric and they all huddled together to discuss what they were going to do next.

Ten minutes later, just as Mr Sparks put his key into the door, he heard a big crash from his workroom; the Button Bear had pushed over a tea tray which made a loud clatter on the floor.

Mr Sparks was so distracted that he rushed in without closing the front door and Cedric and Polo stood at the door and called to the Button Bear, "Come on, run!"

But the Button Bear was so weighed down with buttons he could hardly walk, never mind run.

"Where do you think you're going?" growled Mr Sparks who sprang forward and slammed the door shut, nearly squashing Cedric's snout!

CHAPTER 3

The next day, Cedric and Polo returned to the tailor's workshop and looked inside. The tailor was nowhere to be seen.

They called the Button Bear who slowly moved towards the window. He looked very unhappy.

Cedric was brisk as he felt sure the Button Bear was going to cry. "Look, BB, don't be sad. Polo and I are going to get you out of there, isn't that right, Polo?"

"Absolutely," he nodded.

"But how?" asked the Button Bear with a small voice.

"Firstly, we have to get in there and cut off all those buttons so that you can run faster."

"Oh, okay," said the Button Bear who didn't sound very sure about this.

"But how are you going to get in?"

"Plan B", said Cedric decisively and they huddled together and discussed what they were going to do next.

Several hours later, under a bright full moon, a small line of animals, led by Cedric and Polo, crept along the street where the Button Bear lived. Polo's friends from the zoo, the squirrel monkeys, had happily agreed to help with the plan to rescue the Button Bear and came well equipped with a bag of tools.

"How are we going to remove these bars?" said Cedric, as he tried to pull apart the metal bars that were in front of the window.

"Monkey wrench?" said one of the squirrel monkeys with a cheeky grin as he pulled out the wrench from the tool bag.

"Amazing!" said Cedric, laughing.

Everyone worked together very well, although Polo regularly had to ask the squirrel monkeys to be quiet - they did love to chatter!

In no time at all they had loosened all of the bars so that Cedric was able to pull them out and eventually they climbed down into the tailor's workroom to reach BB.

The Button Bear cried with joy.

"Now," said Cedric, "the next thing we must do is to get all those buttons off. Everyone, we must work fast but we must also be very, very gentle, okay?"

Each of the squirrel monkeys used their excellent teeth to bite through the thread that attached the buttons to the Button Bear whilst Cedric and Polo worked gently with the scissors to snip through the stitches.

"Does it hurt?" asked Cedric kindly.

"No, not too much," said BB.

"There," said Polo as the last button was removed.

The Button Bear looked at each of them and two huge tears fell down his face.

"I can't tell you how good it feels," he said through his tears and he shook each one of them by the paw (and Polo by his flipper) and they all smiled and hugged each other.

Chico, the youngest squirrel monkey was so excited that he jumped up and down throwing all the buttons on the floor.

He made so much noise that he woke up Mr Sparks who came into the room shouting angrily. "What's going on here?! Why you cheeky monkeys! And where's my button bear?"

"I'm over here and you can't catch me!"

The tailor looked at the button bear without his buttons and blinked in astonishment. Then his face got redder and redder as the monkeys jumped out of the window and Polo and Cedric and the button bear dashed for the door!

With surprising speed, the furious tailor lunged towards the button bear but just as he was about to grab him, Mr Sparks slipped and skidded on all the buttons. He looked really funny like a very bad ice skater!

"Ooohhh" this way and "Whoaahh" that way!

Then, he fell backwards with a giant crash.

"Aaargh!" he screamed and shot up again!

"Look!" cried Cedric "He's fallen onto that enormous pin cushion!"

Everyone laughed so much that they even started to cry to see the mean Mr Sparks with lots of pins stuck in the seat of his pyjama pants.

"Ow! Ow! Ow!" he shouted as he ran back into his bedroom trying to remove all the pins.

Cedric and Polo and BB thanked the squirrel monkeys who quickly dashed back to the zoo before anyone could realise they were missing.

"Now that nasty tailor knows how you must have felt, BB," said Polo. "And I better be going home, too. Cedric, I've got another show tomorrow!"

"Thank you so much, Polo! Thank you," said the button bear who gave him a big hug.

And with a wave of his flippers, Polo set off.

"Well," said Cedric, "I think you need to come home with me, BB, and have something to eat. You must be starving – I know I am!"

"Oh, Cedric, you are so kind. Thank you. That would be lovely".

CHAPTER 4

After a delicious meal of spring pie and summer pudding, washed down with marigold tea, Cedric rubbed his ample tummy and turned to BB and said, "Well, my friend, we need to decide what to do next, but let's start at the beginning; how did you come to be with horrible Mr Sparks?"

And so, BB told his sad story which was quite a happy one to begin with.

BB used to live with a Spanish family in Brighton and he was the favourite toy of a little girl called Rosita.

Unfortunately, Rosita had been very sick as a baby which meant that she couldn't speak, so Rosita never gave BB a name. Even so, BB knew that

Rosita loved him because she never went anywhere without him.

One day, the removal men came to the house to pack up all the belongings of Rosita's family because they were moving to London where Rosita's papa had a new job. Well, with all the chaos of so many people packing things up, moving things around with so many boxes everywhere, poor BB got packed in the wrong box! Instead of leaving him out for Rosita, the packing men put him in the box for the charity shop which is where the awful Mr Sparks found him and decided to use poor BB as a button bear.

"Well, BB, I have an idea. We need to go to the Spanish Embassy to talk to Chihuahua."

"A chi-what-wa?"

"No," laughed Cedric. "She's not a chihuahua, that's her name... she's actually a cat! It's a complicated story which I'll tell you another time. Now we need to get some sleep; we have a lot to do tomorrow."

So, Cedric and BB settled down to rest.

Very soon, Cedric was in the deep sleep of a very tired bear, but BB remained awake for a long time, thinking of how strange and wonderful it was to be free.

CHAPTER 5

The following day, Cedric and BB headed for the Spanish Embassy and consulted Chihuahua. She laughed when she saw BB struggling with her name!

"Call me Chi! Everyone does, except for Cedric," she said as she looked at him with a shy smile.

Phew, thought BB. "Thank you, Chi."

"So, I understand your problem, BB, and I think the best thing to do is put out a message on the Embassy social page for a little girl called Rosita who has lost her teddy bear called... BB?"

"Well, said Cedric, that's the name we gave him. He doesn't really have a name."

Cedric and Chi both looked at BB who looked back at them with a tearful expression.

"However, I am sure you do have a real name, BB! Once we find Rosita we will know what it is!"

"Absolutamente!" said Chi. "Just leave it with me and I will get back to you as soon as I hear anything. Okay?"

"Thank you so much," said BB.

"Lovely to see you again, Chihuahua," said Cedric warmly.

Chi flashed a bright smile at Cedric and with a swish of her tail she was gone.

CHAPTER 6

For the next two days, Cedric kept BB as busy as possible to stop him from worrying and wondering when or even if they would get some news from Chi. Each night BB tossed and turned.

What will I do if Chi can't find Rosita? he thought nervously. He would have to make a new life all alone. The idea made BB feel very frightened.

The next day, Chi arrived at Cedric's home. She looked very excited. "Come with me, both of you, hurry!"

Chi turned and dashed towards the park and Cedric and BB rushed after her.

Suddenly, BB felt two small arms around him.

"It's Raul! My Raul! Raul!" the little girl cried with delight.

"Is that Rosita?" said Cedric with astonishment.

"Si!" said a smiling Chi.

"But how did you find her?"

"Well, let's just say I have my contacts... and I had a little help from the Internet! Rosita's family have been looking for Raul ever since they lost him. I spotted his photo on the missing pets' site."

"But I thought that Rosita couldn't speak," said Cedric.

"Ah, well, modern medicine can do wonderful things. A fine doctor fixed that problem easy-peasy!"

The button bear came up to Chi and Cedric with a look of pure joy. "Thank you, Chi, so much for finding my family. And thank you, Cedric, for all you have done for me. You and your kind friends saved me from a terrible life with Mr Sparks. I am so grateful."

"It was my pleasure... Raul!" exclaimed Cedric and gave him a big bear hug.

THE END

PART 3
CEDRIC IN PARIS

CHAPTER 1

As a warm summer breeze fluttered the curtains of the open window, Cedric smiled a contented smile. He was having his breakfast, drinking marigold tea in his favourite cup with an unopened letter on the table.

How nice to get a real letter, thought Cedric. *Email is very efficient, so fast, but actual letters have stamps – and look at this one from France. It's very interesting – and handwritten, so much more personal! I wonder who it's from?*

He muttered to himself as he read the letter and then exclaimed, "My dear cousin, Velours! How wonderful. My goodness, I haven't heard from her for such a long time.

"And what's this?" he said, as something fell out of the envelope.

It was a Eurostar ticket.

Velours had invited Cedric to visit her in Paris!

"Gosh, the ticket's for tomorrow! I better hurry up and pack!"

And with a big slurp of his tea, he dashed to the bedroom.

The following day, Cedric set off bright and early for Kings Cross St Pancras station. He was very excited because he'd never been on the Eurostar before.

When he told his friend, Polo, about his trip, he had urged Cedric to stay awake as the train goes through the tunnel.

"That way", said Polo, "you can see lots of fish swimming in the sea!"

Hmm, thought Cedric, *is that really true? It would be exciting but I think Polo might have been pulling my leg.*

Cedric was thrilled as he rode on the strange, slanting moving walkway leading up to the platform. Then he gasped as he saw the train; it was like a giant, silver, purring serpent that went on forever!

All the passengers scurried around, some laughing and chattering happily, others looking anxious and confused whilst the smart and kind attendants swiftly guided them left and right until everyone was on board.

Cedric sat back in his seat and smiled contentedly.

As the announcement came over the intercom to say that they were now entering the channel tunnel, Cedric couldn't help staring at the window in case he would actually see the sea. But all he saw was darkness and all he heard was the loud rumbling of the train. The rhythm of the train began to make him sleepy and his head nodded.

Then, all of a sudden, he saw hundreds of brightly coloured fish swimming in every direction, but perhaps he was only dreaming.

CHAPTER 2

"We will soon be arriving at Gare du Nord, please take all of your luggage with you and thank you for travelling on Eurostar!" said the voice over the intercom.

Cedric stirred in his seat, rubbed his eyes with his paws and leant forward excitedly.

Everyone was hurrying and getting ready to get off, but Cedric waited as he preferred not to join the rush.

Humans are so impatient, thought Cedric, who liked to feel relaxed and calm. *Besides, what can be so urgent that they have to act as if the train was on fire?*

Cedric was the last to get off the train and, as he stepped onto the platform, he heard a great echoing clamour of a busy railway station.

Cedric felt the excitement he always felt when he came to Paris. And best of all, he was so happy to know that he would see Velours very soon. He felt sure he would recognise her but he had to admit that it was a very long time since they had seen each other.

But Velours has a velvet coat of the deepest, darkest blue, like no other cat in all the world. I'm sure I will recognise her.

When Cedric got to the end of the platform, he looked left, then right and then he looked straight ahead, but he couldn't see any sign of Velours.

So, he found a bench, sat himself down and waited. Suddenly, everything went dark as two velvety paws covered his eyes and a voice behind him said, "Coucou, Cedric!"

"Velours! How wonderful to see you!" cried Cedric and he jumped up to give her a great big bear hug which was so snuggly because of Cedric's own fine fabric and Velours soft velvet coat.

"Ah, Velours, you look exactly the same... oh! But, Velours, what happened? What happened to your leg?" said Cedric sadly looking down at the place where Velours' back left leg should have been; in its place was a rubber wheel.

"Yes, well, that is a bit of a long story... why don't we go to my home and I will tell you all about it. Cher Cedric, don't look so sad. It happened a long time ago now and I am quite used to it. I prefer to focus on what I have, you know? Look, I can go even faster now!"

Velours sprinted along the train platform, did the most amazing twirl on the wheel that replaced her back left paw, and sped forward towards Cedric coming to a scorching stop inches from Cedric's feet.

"Wow! You really are fast. That was incredible!"

CHAPTER 3

After a short journey on the metro, Velours led the way into a quiet street in a very old part of Paris. They stopped at a tall, elegant house and passed into the garden where there was a shed.

Velours opened the door and, with a big smile, turned to Cedric, "Welcome to my home! Do you like it?"

"It's wonderful, Velours!" said Cedric as he took in the colourful sight of bright, exotic fabrics, with strings of coloured lights, plump floor cushions and a hammock.

Velours hopped into the hammock and said, "This is my favourite spot, especially because at night I can look through the skylight at the stars."

Cedric looked up and agreed it was a fine feature.

"And while you are here, you can have the hammock – I insist!"

Cedric was actually a little uncertain about the hammock, but he didn't like to say so.

"Now, shall I make you some supper and... some marigold tea?"

"Oh, Velours, you remembered! Yes, please. And

then you can tell me your news, but first of all, please tell me what happened to your leg."

Velours prepared a delicious meal and after they sat down to eat, she began to tell the story of her accident.

"It was about two years ago, I was talking a stroll with my friend Capitaine who lives near Notre Dame, when suddenly, out of nowhere, an aggressive cyclist who was too impatient to wait for the traffic lights to change, left the road and started cycling on the pavement. He was going at full speed and shouting at everyone to get out of his way. Well, I was looking at a shop window and I didn't see the cyclist until the last moment when he was almost on top of me! Capitaine barked loudly to warn me but it was too late. I tried to jump out of the way but the cyclist ran over my back-left paw.

Oooh, Cedric, it was soooo painful, I screamed and then, well, I don't remember much more until I came around on the operating table of a very kind vet called Roget Bonhomme. My previous owners were not very kind! Can you believe it? They didn't want to take me home with just three paws and told Roget to put me to sleep! Quel horreur!"

"How horrible!" said Cedric, dropping his cake into his tea in shock.

"So, this very nice man, Roget Bonhomme - a perfect name for him, don't you think? It means Roger Good Man in English - he decided to keep me and help me. It was Roget who came up with the idea of replacing my damaged paw with a wheel, and as we French say, 'Voila'!

And then Roget heard of the gentleman who owns this shed and the house, Gilbert Gentilhomme, and I was offered a home here. Gilbert is a very kind person but I do worry about him. He works so hard. He is very rich, but I am not sure he has a lot of fun, you know. He always looks so stressed. I'm trying to help him to look after himself more. And you, Cedric, tell me some news about you!"

Cedric opened his mouth to speak and was embarrassed when a big yawn came out.

"Oh, Cedric, you are so tired! Let's unpack your things and you can rest."

Cedric gratefully agreed.

"Now, Cedric, I need to go out for a training run; Le Grand Dash is only a couple of days away."

"Sorry, Le Grand Dash – what is that?"

"Oh, quel idiot I am! I didn't explain, did I? Well, it's a big race, but I'll tell you all about it later, okay?"

And with that, Velours hopped out of the door and out into the street.

Cedric looked at the hammock and attempted to get in. He got in, and then he fell out. He tried from the other side. He managed to get in, with his shoulders up close to his ears, then he tried to turn on his side, and fell out. Then he tried from the top end, pulling a chair close to the hammock to steady himself and, hey presto, that worked.

In less than a blink he was fast asleep.

As he dreamed, he turned on his side – and fell out.

When Velours returned from her training run, she covered her mouth to stop herself from laughing out loud as she saw poor Cedric sleeping on the floor with one paw still in the hammock. She pushed some cushions together and gently rolled Cedric onto them and then covered him with a light cotton blanket.

A little while later, she hopped into the hammock and fell fast asleep.

CHAPTER 4

The next morning, during a delicious breakfast, Velours explained to Cedric about her part in Le Grand Dash.

"When I lost my back leg, Cedric, it took me some time to adjust to it. I was having some rehabilitation – do you know what that is?"

"Yes, it's exercise and treatment to help you to recover, isn't it?"

"Correct. During this time, it became clear that I was really quite fast and someone suggested I try out for the Pet Paralympics which I did. Le Grand Dash is one of the key races in the Pet Paralympics and it takes place in two days' time. I hope you don't think me big-headed if I tell you that I am actually the favourite to win!"

"Velours, you are truly amazing! I am so impressed. Can I watch the race?"

"But of course, Cedric, it's why I wanted to invite you here. In fact, I hope you can help me a little with my training today. Can you ride a bicycle?"

Later that day, Cedric and Velours were sitting in a café near Notre Dame with Capitaine.

Cedric was laughing as he explained how he tried to help Velours with her training, but in fact, she was going faster than him!

"Anyway, Cedric, it still helped me. And we had a lot of fun, oui?"

Then Velours turned to Capitaine, "Capitaine, why don't you tell Cedric about your job?"

Capitaine was a very distinguished golden retriever. He explained to Cedric that he used to be in the army, but now he worked as a support pet. He was trained to help his diabetic master, Olivier.

Olivier was, unfortunately, in a wheelchair because of his diabetes so Capitaine helped him with practical tasks at home, fetching things for him – even helping him to take off his socks! Most importantly of all,

Capitaine had to watch out for signs that Olivier might be having a 'hypo' (it means he needs to have some apple juice very quickly because his blood sugar is dangerously low). When this happened, Capitaine was able to warn Olivier by barking loudly and standing at the fridge where the fruit juice was kept.

"You see, Cedric," said Velours, "what an important job this is?"

"Oh, indeed, I do. We have assistance pets in the UK, too; it's essential work. Well done, Capitaine."

"Merci, Cedric. And speaking of my job, I need to return to Olivier. See you at the race. Bonne chance, Velours, but I feel you don't really need it! I'm sure you're going to win!"

CHAPTER 5

Finally, the day of the Le Grand Dash had arrived. Paris woke to bright sunshine and an air of excitement. All along the Champs Elysées, Pet Paralympians from across the world were making their final preparations for the afternoon's race.

As Velours was doing her own warm-up exercises in the park, Cedric was alone when Capitaine arrived, looking very worried.

"What's wrong, Capitaine?"

As Capitaine didn't know Cedric well, he hesitated.

"Please tell me, maybe I can help. Two heads are better than one, Capitaine."

He thanked Cedric and told him; his master, Olivier, was missing. He had gone out using his electric wheelchair to his bank and he didn't come back.

"And then there was this, Cedric," and he played a message on his mobile phone.

They listened to a strange recording of Olivier sounding confused and then the phone cut out.

"He's in trouble, Cedric, and he may be having a hypo - and I don't know where he is!"

"Surely we can track him using the phone?" said Cedric.

"Usually, but I can't pick up a signal for him. I am very worried, frankly speaking."

Then Velours joined them and Capitaine told her the situation.

"Well, let's put our heads together and see what we can do!"

"Ah, Velours, that is very kind, but don't forget you have your race today."

"Listen, Capitaine, this is more important, isn't it? The race is just a race compared to the danger Olivier is in. We can find him, I'm sure!" said Velours with a bright smile.

"Yes, three heads are even better than two!"

"You are right, Cedric, but why stop at three? We must call all our friends and get them to help as well."

Capitaine had regained his military composure and took the lead. Between them, Capitaine and Velours called everyone they knew and ask them to contact everyone they knew. Soon, they had dogs and cats across the whole of Paris looking for Olivier.

Velours went in one direction and Capitaine asked Cedric to search with him. As soon as they were alone, Capitaine turned to Cedric and said, "Cedric, I know Velours said that she doesn't mind about the race but I know that's not true; she was just being kind. She has worked so hard for this. I want her to run in Le Grand Dash; this is her best chance to win it."

"I can see you have a plan, Capitaine, tell me what you want me to do."

"Great. What I want you to do is to delay the race."

"Wow! Okay. Any idea how I can do that?"

"No, my friend, I just want to ask you to try – I must focus on my master, I am so afraid for him."

Cedric saw that Capitaine was close to tears, but he was far too proud to cry.

"Leave it with me," said, Cedric. "You go and look for Olivier."

Capitaine hugged Cedric and, with a grateful smile, left him standing alone on the pavement.

Cedric rested his chin upon his chest and thought hard for a few moments.

Then, decisively, he went back to the shed to collect Velours' bike and headed for the starting line of Le Grand Dash.

CHAPTER 6

The Champs Elysées' pavements were crowded with people and pets all waiting for the start of the race.

The Pet Paralympians, dogs and cats of all breeds, all disabilities hovered on the starting line, hopping and twitching with nervous energy, some wheelchair racers crouched close to the ground ready to spring forward.

"Stoooopp!" cried Cedric as he pedalled towards the great Dane who was about to sound the klaxon to start the race.

"Arret!" he cried again in French.

Everyone stared at the strange bear pedalling

furiously towards Oskar, the great Dane.

"Monsieur Bear," said Oskar, "this is not the Tour de France! What are you doing?"

Quickly Cedric explained that Velours was not ready to run because she was helping with the search for Olivier.

Oskar turned to the Pet Paralympians and said solemnly, "Pet Paralympians, we have a serious dilemma regarding our colleague, Velours. She is doing her public duty and helping to find a human master who is in serious danger. If you all agree, we will delay the race by one hour. Please raise your paw if you agree."

Everyone talked for a few moments and one by one they raised their paws.

"Excuse me!" came the sharp voice of a wheelchair

poodle from the back of the pack, "I do not agree! I withhold my consent!"

Everyone else turned to look at Viola, the poodle, as she turned to Oskar with a fierce expression on her face. "We are ready to go! If we wait for Velours, we will not be at our peak condition and you should not make a special case for her."

Minnie, a Burmese blue cat, whispered to the Pekinese beside her and said, "I know why she doesn't want to wait; she knows that she can't beat Velours! Besides which, Viola is a cheat!"

Chen, the Pekinese looked shocked and was about to ask Minnie what she meant, when Oskar announced, sadly, "In accordance with the rules of the Pet Paralympian Committee, one objection means we must go ahead with the race as planned."

Oskar began to go up the starter's platform when Cedric, realising he had to try something else, set off on the bike, zig-zagging across the race course! Oskar couldn't start the race, and with a small smile he stepped back down off the podium.

All the Pet Paralympians – with the exception of a furious Viola whose white poodle curls were turning pink at the edges, she was so cross – clapped and shouted, "Go, Cedric!"

The police and the support vehicles looked on in surprise and then began to chase Cedric. For a little while he was able to avoid them, zipping back and forwards, from side to side, but in the end, they were too fast for him.

One police officer grabbed Cedric and his bike and was about to put them into his police van. Cedric tried desperately to explain why Velours could not be there, but he was so out of breath that he could barely speak. He managed to say Capitaine's name and the police dog beside the arresting officer barked loudly.

"Wait!" shouted Hero, "I know Capitaine, we were at Military school together. Let's hear what Cedric has to say."

So, with a halting voice, Cedric explained that Olivier was in danger and must be found as soon as possible.

The police officer took immediate control and, using Cedric's phone, called Capitaine for an update.

Then, going up to Oskar, he asked to borrow the megaphone, ran up the steps of the starter's podium and said, "Dear Pet Paralympians and Humans, one of our French brothers is missing and in great danger. We police cannot stay here while you race, so, I am desolated but you cannot run Le Grand Dash right now. Moreover, I want to ask your help in finding Olivier, who is a diabetic and a wheelchair user – just like some of you, Pet Paralympians. Please help us to find him. He may be having a hypo, and may even have been attacked. Will you give us one hour? We can put a replacement police team to support the race in place by then. You can run at three o'clock, no later. Do you agree?"

"Oui!" came the loud reply, with lots of barking and waving paws.

"Excellent. This is the true spirit of the Olympics! So, if you look at the big screen over there, you can see Olivier's photograph. Allez!"

The Pet Paralympians shot off in all directions and the police set off on their motorbikes.

Cedric looked around him unsure of where to go because he didn't know Paris very well. Minnie the Burmese Blue turned to him and said, "I'm Minnie, and this is Chen, what's your name?"

"It's Cedric."

"Okay, do you want to come with us, Cedric? We can search together."

Cedric, with a grateful smile, hopped back on his bike whilst Minnie and Chen led the way.

Not very far away, Capitaine was searching near the Rue de Rivoli where Olivier's bank was located but there was no sign of Olivier. He tried Olivier's phone again, but it went straight to voicemail which normally it would never do. It was agreed that masters and their support pets always picked up each other's call.

Capitaine felt more and more afraid. It was well past the time for Olivier to have his medication, and besides, something else had clearly happened; *who was it that was shouting at Olivier just before the phone cut off?*

Capitaine headed for the Tuileries Gardens, perhaps Olivier had gone there?

Suddenly, all the hairs on Capitaine's neck stood on end and a strong scent filled his nostrils. He began to run! He knew from the scent that his master was somewhere closeby! Yes, in the direction of the café... but where?

There he was!

Capitaine dashed up to him and knew immediately that Olivier was unwell.

"Hey, stop that barking," said the waiter. "Is this your master? He's been mumbling and grumbling and not making any sense! Is he drunk?"

Quel idiot! thought Capitaine, and shouted, "He's having a hypo!"

"A what?" asked the waiter.

"A diabetic attack!" shouted Capitaine. "He needs apple juice, quickly!"

Finally, the waiter understood and with a surprising turn of speed dashed to the fridge and grabbed some apple juice, forcing it into Olivier's mouth.

"Good, good…" said Capitaine who had in the meantime called an ambulance. And then he rang Velours.

"You've found him! Oh, thank goodness! Bravo! Is he okay, Capitaine?"

"He will be, Velours. The ambulance is here now. Velours, please go and run your race. Go and win, my dear!!"

When Cedric, Minnie and Chen heard the good news, they hugged each other and dashed back to the Champs Elysées.

Velours, however, was still quite far away.

Oskar was checking the time. "We simply must start the race at three o'clock," he said to one of the other officials.

Minnie and Chen were back at the start line. Viola, the poodle, was in front of them.

Chen whispered to Minnie, "Why did you say that Viola is a cheat? That's a very serious thing to say, Minnie."

"Yes, it is a serious thing to say and I would never say such a thing without any evidence."

Then, in a loud voice, Minnie said, "If you look closely at the rear wheel of her chair, Chen, you can see a small metal box..."

"Oh, yes, I can see it. What is it? Goodness me! It's a motor!" cried Chen.

Viola didn't move a muscle, nor did she turn around, but the edges of her white fur had turned very pink once more.

Minnie looked at Chen and said, "I told you!"

Chen looked really cross. "That's terrible! That's not in the spirit of the Olympics! We should do something, Minnie!"

Minnie smiled and said, "Yes, we will, later. Look."

And Chen turned to see Viola wheeling her chair away from the start line of Le Grand Dash.

"We can file a report with the Pet Paralympian Committee, but now we need to run. Where is Velours?"

Just then, a police van with its horn blaring rushed up to the start line and out jumped Velours! Everyone cheered!

"Okay, Pet Paralympians, prepare yourselves,"

called Oskar, and then he sounded the klaxon and they were off.

The crowd roared. Le Grand Dash had begun.

The racers tore along the Champs Elysées for the premier speed race of the Pet Paralympics.

Disabled cats and dogs of various breeds were all equal in this race. Fur was flying, tails were wagging, paws pounded the ground and wheels squealed. Soon it was a two-pet race, Velours was at the front leading all the way, but close behind was Heidi, a German Shepherd tracker dog.

Faster and faster they ran! Closer and closer came Heidi!

Velours didn't look back but knew in her fur that Heidi was only inches away.

The winning line was shimmering white in the sunlight drawing them both on as they pushed their bodies to their limit.

Now Heidi was shoulder to shoulder with Velours!

Velours hit the tape – and so did Heidi at exactly the same time!

It was a dead-heat.

The crowd roared.

What a race.

Cedric rushed towards Velours and scooped her up in the biggest, snuggliest hug.

"Well done, Velours, you've won!"

CHAPTER 7

After the race, Cedric and Capitaine returned to Velours' home. They celebrated with marigold tea and a special cake made by Capitaine.

Velours was extremely tired, but very happy. They were admiring the gold Champion's medal which Velours was wearing.

Then Velours said, "And Olivier is going to be okay, Capitaine? What happened?"

"Yes, don't worry, the hospital will keep him in for a couple of days. He was mugged, Velours. After he withdrew his money from the bank, he went for a coffee in the Tuileries Gardens. The robbers must have followed him from the bank. He was using his phone to call me when they grabbed his wallet off him. Then they hit him and took his phone. The doctor thinks the shock brought on the hypo."

Capitaine looked serious for a moment, remembering.

Then Cedric turned to Velours and asked, "But tell me, Velours, are you a bit sad that you had to share your prize with Heidi instead of winning Le Grand Dash outright?"

"Ah, you know I am very competitive, and if it had been anyone else, well, I would have been very disappointed. However, Heidi has a very special connection to me. Heidi is a mountain tracker dog and several years ago she saved the life of Roget Bonhomme when he got caught in an avalanche in Grenoble. Alors, Heidi saved Roget and Roget saved me! I can't think of a better result, can you?"

THE END

The story of Cedric's creation

Cedric the bear is the original creation of Katie Eggington (nee Mantell).

Both Cedric and Katie were featured in the BBC programme, Paul Martin's Handmade Revolution in 2012. Katie was one of the winning designers and Cedric was proudly displayed in the V&A Museum shop.

On seeing the programme, Lucia Wilson decided to approach Katie to discuss creating a series of children's stories based on Cedric. Anne Bowes (a talented illustrator and jewellery designer) joined the project and has created some delightful illustrations.

Lucia, Katie and Anne worked together to bring Cedric to life in these three stories.

Liesbeth Heenk at Amsterdam Publishers was the final link to us realising their dream of having these stories published. The Adventures of Cedric the Bear is now available worldwide.

Katie Eggington – Original Creator of Cedric

Katie Eggington is the designer and creative force behind Creative Threads. Having graduated from Norwich University of the Arts with a first class BA (hons) in Textiles, Katie carved out a unique product in her distinctive handmade teddy bears. Working from her home studio in Hampshire, Katie meticulously designs and brings to life each bear individually. Katie spends many hours with each bear, every part of the process being completed by hand including weaving each bear's fabric on her hand loom. Katie's wider collection of work has also earned its place in the media spotlight, with features in publications including the Dorset Echo, Eastern Daily Press, and the NUA Alumni Magazine. Katie now shares her wealth of weave experience and knowledge with the next generation through her technical weave blog Creative Threads: creative-threads.co.uk.

Lucia Wilson – Author of the Cedric book

Lucia Wilson is a British-born Anglo-Burmese writer of poetry, lyrics and stories for all ages. She is a member of SACEM and PRS and lives in London. Lucia's novella, The Karloff Tiara, is available on Amazon. In the summer of 2016, Lucia decided to ask Katie if she would like to collaborate on a series of children's books about Cedric and this led to the creation of "Cedric at the Museum","Cedric and the Button Bear" and "Cedric in Paris" with illustrations by Anne Bowes.

Anne Bowes – Illustrator of the Cedric book

Anne Bowes is an artist and jewellery designer based in East Sussex and London. She studied Decorative Arts and Textiles at Camberwell School of Art before going on to a career in graphic design and illustration. Anne created her jewellery brand Anne Bowes: annebowesjewellery.com.